DEXTER BEXLEY
AND THE BIG
BLUE BEASTIE

In memory of Spook,
who knew when to go

DEXTER BEXLEY AND THE BIG BLUE BEASTIE
A DOUBLEDAY BOOK 978 0 385 61005 6

Published in Great Britain by Doubleday,
an imprint of Random House Children's Books

This edition published 2007

1 3 5 7 9 10 8 6 4 2

Copyright ©Joel Stewart, 2007

Set in Joel 1 Regular

RANDOM HOUSE CHILDREN'S BOOKS
61–63 Uxbridge Road, London W5 5SA
A division of The Random House Group Ltd

RANDOM HOUSE AUSTRALIA (PTY) LTD
20 Alfred Street, Milsons Point, Sydney,
New South Wales 2061, Australia

RANDOM HOUSE NEW ZEALAND LTD
18 Poland Road, Glenfield, Auckland 10, New Zealand

RANDOM HOUSE (PTY) LTD
Isle of Houghton, Corner Boundary Road & Carse O'Gowrie, Houghton 2198, South Africa

THE RANDOM HOUSE GROUP Limited Reg. No. 954009
www.kidsatrandomhouse.co.uk

A CIP catalogue record for this book is available from the British Library.

Printed and bound in Singapore

DEXTER BEXLEY
AND THE BIG
THE
BLUE BEASTIE

JOEL STEWART

DOUBLEDAY

Dexter Bexley scooted . . .

. . . and scooted.

Right into . . .

. . . a Big Blue Beastie!

But Dexter Bexley had a much better idea.

Dexter Bexley and the Big Blue Beastie scooted . . .

. . . and scooted, until . . .

Dexter Bexley and the Big Blue Beastie

went into business

delivering flowers.

Dexter Bexley and the Big Blue Beastie gave up the flower delivery business and became . . .

BEXLEY AND BEAST:
Private Detectives.

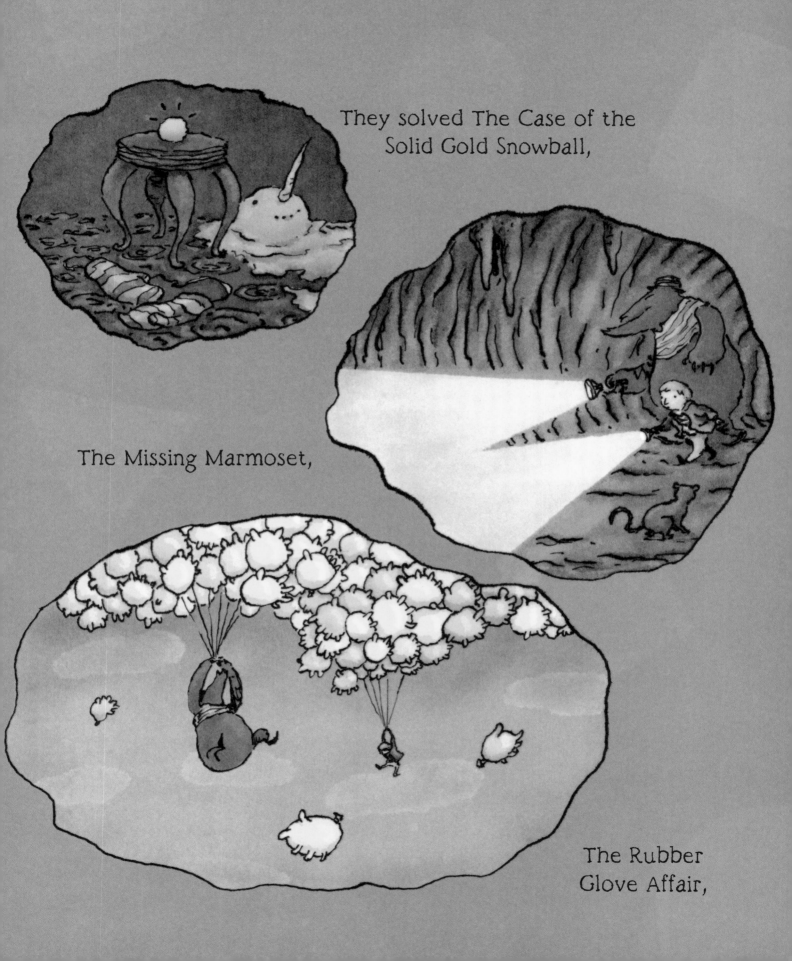

They solved The Case of the
Solid Gold Snowball,

The Missing Marmoset,

The Rubber
Glove Affair,

The Bicycle from Beyond

and The Great Sausage Heist.

They even apprehended their arch nemesis, Professor Hortern Zoar.

Though he later escaped.

Dexter Bexley invented the biggest, stickiest,
tastiest Yoghurt, Fudge, Banana, Ice-creamy
Beastie Feast ever!

Really, it was huge!

But for once Dexter Bexley
was clean out of ideas.

"I'M CLEAN OUT OF IDEAS,"

said Dexter Bexley.

"I SUPPOSE NOW
YOU'LL **HAVE** TO EAT ME UP."

The Big Blue Beastie bought himself
a very gooey lollipop.

And one for Dexter Bexley.

... NOW THAT I'VE FOUND A FRIEND."

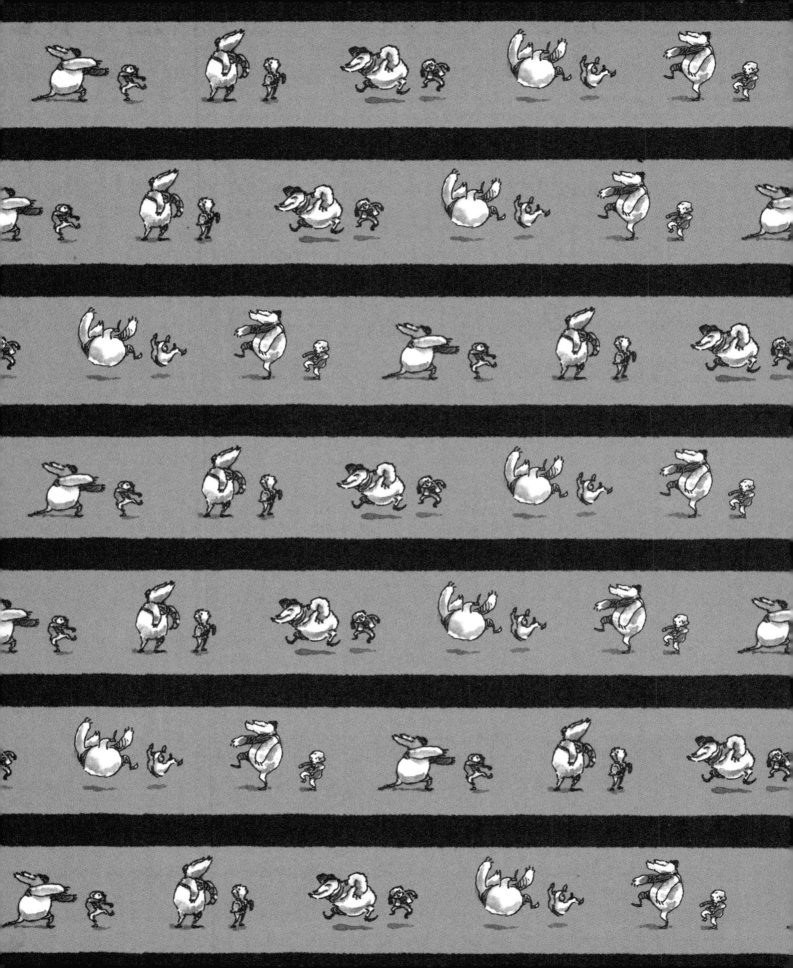